A
"Thinking of Others"
BOOK

Ivy's Icicle

✳ ✳ ✳

BOOK THREE
Forgiving Others

✳ ✳ ✳

Written by GARY BOWER
Illustrated by JAN BOWER

TYNDALE KiDS

TYNDALE HOUSE PUBLISHERS, INC. WHEATON, ILLINOIS

Acknowledgments

It was a thrill to work with my family on this project. I am amazed at how my wife always turns such hard work into unforgettable fun. I am particularly grateful to all my children, who inspired me to write this story by how readily they forgive each other. I also want to thank those who offered excellent suggestions, and my son Austin for his perseverance in building a snowman out of uncooperative snow.

— GARY BOWER

I am very thankful for my daughter Jasmine, an extremely forgiving person who eagerly posed as Ivy and effortlessly portrayed such a wide array of emotions. My gratitude also goes to my daughter Angel, who, as Emily, added a sweetness to many of the illustrations, and to Levi Norris (Dustin), Pete Norris (Dad), and Gerry Harris (Grandma).

— JAN BOWER

Visit Tyndale's exciting Web site at www.tyndale.com

Ivy's Icicle

Text copyright © 2002 by Gary D. Bower. All rights reserved.

Cover and interior illustrations copyright © 2002 by Jan Bower. All rights reserved.

Photo of Gary and Jan Bower copyright © 2002 by G. Bower. All rights reserved.

Scripture quotations are taken from *The Living Bible,* copyright © 1971. Used by permission of Tyndale House Publishers, Inc., Wheaton, Illinois 60189. All rights reserved.

Library of Congress Cataloging-in-Publication Data

Bower, Gary.
  Ivy's icicle / written by Gary Bower ; illustrated by Jan Bower.
    p. cm.
"A thinking of others book, book three: forgiving others."
Summary: Ivy is very upset when her brother accidentally breaks the doll
Grandma had given her for Christmas, but she eventually learns how to
forgive him.
  ISBN 0-8423-7417-5 (alk. paper)
  [1. Grandmothers--Fiction. 2. Brothers and sisters--Fiction. 3.
Forgiveness--Fiction.] I. Bower, Jan, ill. II. Title.
  PZ7.B6753 Iv 2002
  [E]--dc21
                          2002008941

Printed in China
09 08 07 06 05 04 03 02
10 9 8 7 6 5 4 3 2 1

For the many warmhearted people
who have forgiven me through the years.

I vy gazed out the dining-room window. "When are they going to come?" she asked.

"Any minute," Mom said. "Your dad called and said the flight was right on time." She glanced at the table. "Forks go on the left, Ivy. Remember?"

"Oops," said Ivy.

While Ivy rearranged the silverware, two bright headlights beamed through the window. Light danced around the room, making the dishes sparkle.

Ivy's little sister, Emily, scampered to the door, clapping her hands. "Nana's here! Nana's here!"

Bells jingled and snow swirled into the house when the door swung open. Dad helped Grandma step out of the cold air as sounds of laughter and stomping of boots filled the happy room.

Ivy's brother, Dustin, galloped down the stairs. "Grandma!" he shouted.

Emily couldn't stop bouncing up and down. "Nana! Nana!" she giggled.

For a moment, Ivy acted shy. Then she rushed to Grandma and hugged her like she'd never let go.

"What a warm welcome!" Grandma chuckled. "Now, let me have a look at you."

She stepped back and peeked over the top of her glasses. "My, how my Ivy has grown!" she said.

A grin spread across Ivy's face. Grandma always said that when she came to visit.

Dinner was wonderful. "Everything looks so nice," said Grandma.

"Ivy set the table," said Mom.

Grandma sipped her tea. "So grown up," she said.

After dinner, the children gave Grandma presents they had made. She gave them presents too.

Emily got a ballerina dress. She squealed and twirled with glee.

Dustin tore into his present like a hungry wolf. Then he became quiet.

Grandma had knitted him a sweater. "Thank you," he said politely.

Ivy also got a sweater. "Oh, Grandma, I love it!" she said, holding it up.

"Hmm," said Grandma. "I hope it fits. I can't believe how you've grown, child!"

Ivy began to pick up pieces of wrapping paper. "Not so fast," Grandma told her. "I have another gift for each of you."

Emily's second present was a cuddly pink lamb. She buried her smile in its soft wool.

Dustin perked up when he opened his. "A basketball!" he exclaimed. "Thanks, Grandma!"

Ivy slowly peeled the wrapping paper off her present. Then she gasped. Staring at her was the most beautiful porcelain doll she had ever seen.

She was so happy that she could hardly speak. *"Thank you!"* she finally managed to whisper.

Ivy loved Christmas. She loved Grandma. She loved her new doll.

"I'll name you Hannah," she said.

The next day, Ivy had a tea party with Emily.

"Do lambs like tea?" Emily asked.

"I suppose so," Ivy replied.

"Not me," said Emily. "I like chocolate milk."

Ivy carefully took her porcelain doll from the shelf where she had set it the night before.

"Won't you join us for tea, Hannah?" she said very properly.

She pretended to pour the tea for her doll and then turned to Emily. "Tea?"

"Chocolate milk!" said Emily.

"Chocolate milk, *please,*" Ivy corrected her.

"Chocolate milk, *please,*" Emily said.

As Ivy passed a cup to Emily, Dustin entered the room. He bounced his basketball with a loud *thud-thud-thud* on the carpeted floor.

"Didn't Mom say not to bounce the ball in the house?" Ivy reminded him.

Dustin stopped immediately. "I forgot," he said. "But watch this."

He gave the ball a quick spin and tried to balance it on his finger. But it spun away from him and landed with a crash right in the middle of the tea party.

"DUSTIN!" Ivy shrieked.

"I didn't mean it!" Dustin stammered. "It was an accident!"

Ivy looked at the mess. She could hardly believe her eyes. One of Hannah's tiny porcelain hands had broken off.

Ivy tried not to cry, but she just couldn't help it. She burst into tears.

It took only a few minutes for Mom to glue Hannah's hand back on. Dustin watched from across the room. "I'm sorry," he said over and over.

"There," said Mom, setting the doll on its shelf. "When the glue dries it will be like new."

Tearfully, Ivy examined her doll. She could still see a thin, faint crack.

It will never be like new, she thought.

Mom took Dustin's basketball away from him. His head hung low as he followed her out of the room.

"I hope he never gets it back," Ivy said to herself.

She felt miserable. How could he be so careless? Of course, Dustin didn't mean to break her doll; but he *did* break it, and saying he was sorry a hundred times wasn't going to fix it. And the more Ivy pouted about what Dustin had done, the more miserable she felt.

That afternoon, Ivy and her friends Megan and Jenna made a snowman in Ivy's yard. Nearby, Dustin and his friends Aaron and Wyatt threw snowballs at each other.

"What should we use for the snowman's eyes?" Ivy asked.

"How about these?" said Megan. She twisted two pinecones into the snowman's face.

"We can give him a pinecone mouth, too," said Ivy.

"And buttons," said Jenna. "But what can we use for his nose?"

"Maybe a carrot?" Megan suggested.

Ivy looked up at her house. "Or an icicle," she said. All the girls looked up. Long, slender icicles hung from the edge of the roof.

"They're awfully high," Jenna said. "I don't think we can reach them."

"Maybe the boys can," said Megan.

Ivy scowled. "I don't want Dustin to come near my snowman," she said coldly. "He ruins *everything!*"

But the girls couldn't get the icicles to fall, so Dustin, Aaron,
and Wyatt came over to help. Dustin knocked one down with
a snowball on his first try.

"Thank you," said Megan and Jenna.

Ivy didn't say anything. She wouldn't even look at her brother.

The sun sank slowly behind a hill, and one by one the children said good-bye. Little stars speckled the darkening sky as Ivy trudged through the deep snow to her front porch. The wintry evening felt so peaceful that she didn't feel like going inside yet.

Besides, she thought, *Dustin's in there.*

The snowman caught her eye. Its long, icy nose pointed straight at her. It looked yummy.

She plucked the icicle from the snowman's face and sucked on the end of it. It felt cold against her lips. Suddenly, Ivy felt cold all over. She shivered.

She noticed the shimmering white Christmas lights that wrapped around a pine tree by the porch. Their soft glow made her feel warmer.

For a long time she just looked at the lights and thought. She thought about Christmas and Grandma. She thought about how much she liked her presents, especially her doll.

Then she thought about what Dustin had done.

She shivered again.

Why did he have to break my doll? she wondered as she made her way to the door.

After supper, the family sat in the living room. Mom looked at a magazine and Grandma knitted while Dad read a story to Emily. A crackling fire in the fireplace made the room as warm as toast.

"Want to play checkers, Ivy?" Dustin asked.

"Not with you," she mumbled coldly. Her words surprised her. She glanced around the room, hoping no one else had heard.

"The end," said Dad, closing the book. He got up and carried Emily to the window. "Look at those big icicles," he said. "They need to come down, don't you think?"

"Yep," said Emily.

"But they're so pretty, Dad," said Ivy. "Do you have to knock them down?"

"Heavy icicles are dangerous," Dad replied. "They can hurt people. They aren't good for the roof, either."

"Do we need more insulation, Dad?" Dustin asked.

Ivy rolled her eyes. *He thinks he's so smart,* she thought.

"What's *insulation?*" asked Emily.

Grandma held up her knitting. "It's like a sweater that keeps a house warm."

"That's right," Dad agreed. "Icicles are a sign that we're losing heat."

"Mercy!" said Grandma, smiling at Ivy. "Let's not lose our heat. We certainly don't want to grow cold, do we?"

Ivy looked away. She wondered if Grandma had heard what she'd said to Dustin.

Upstairs, as the girls were getting ready for bed, Emily ran to the bedroom window and pointed.

"Look at that big one!"

Ivy looked. Just outside her window hung the biggest icicle she had ever seen. It glowed in the moonlight.

"Is Daddy going to knock it down?" Emily asked.

"Yes," said Ivy.

"Good," said Emily, scampering to her bed. "Big icicles can hurt people."

Emily fell asleep right away, but Ivy couldn't. She felt guilty about how she had spoken to Dustin, but she wasn't sorry. Then she felt guilty for not being sorry.

Her heart wasn't warm toward Dustin like it used to be, and she knew it. It felt like a cold, heavy icicle was growing inside her.

Dad's words echoed in her ears:

"Those icicles need to come down."

Ivy closed her eyes. In her mind she pictured an icicle.

The imaginary icicle grew bigger and bigger, heavier and heavier, until it seemed like its weight would pull the roof down. She imagined trying again and again to hit it with snowballs, but the icicle just wouldn't come down.

She thought about Dustin. It bothered her how easily he had knocked down an icicle, and something inside her started to feel very cold again.

I wish I had a sweater for my heart, she thought.

In the morning, Ivy went to Grandma's room. The door was open, so she peeked inside.

"Grandma?"

The room was quiet. Grandma's shawl and a pair of white gloves were draped over the back of a chair. An old mirror sat on the dresser. Next to the mirror sat Grandma's glasses and lots of other interesting things.

Without hesitating, Ivy clipped on some earrings and looked in the mirror. Then she tried on the shawl, gloves, and glasses.

"My, how you've grown!" she said playfully.

A noise startled her. Quickly, she took off the glasses. But as she tried to take off the earrings, her elbow bumped the glasses. Off the dresser they fell with a clatter against the hard floor.

When Ivy bent down to get them, she was horrified. Grandma's glasses lay in two pieces.

She picked up the pieces and turned around. In the doorway stood Grandma.

"I'm so sorry, Grandma!" Ivy sobbed, showing her the pieces.

But instead of scolding her, Grandma pulled Ivy close and hugged her tightly. She said nothing at all as Ivy cried in her arms.

Finally, Ivy dried her eyes. "Aren't you angry?" she sniffled.

"No, dear," came a gentle reply. "I forgive you."

Rays of sunshine poured through the window, making icicles sparkle like diamonds. *Drip, drip, drip.* They were starting to melt.

Something was melting in Ivy's heart, too. She began to understand how badly Dustin must have felt when he broke her doll's hand, and for the first time in two days she felt sorry for someone besides herself.

At that moment, Ivy made a decision.

I'm going to forgive him.

Grandma's soft voice interrupted her thoughts. "Icicles will certainly come down on a sunny day like this."

Ivy smiled. "One already has," she said.

A few minutes later, Ivy saw Dustin in the living room.

"Do you want to play checkers?" she asked.

Dustin looked surprised. "Uh . . . sure," he said.

The children set up the checkerboard.

"You can go first," Ivy said cheerfully.

Dustin paused. "I'm really sorry about what I did to your doll," he said.

"I know," said Ivy, "and I forgive you. Will you forgive me for being so mean last night?"

Dustin moved a checker. "Of course," he said. "It's your turn."

Near the end of the day, Ivy stood by Grandma's rocking chair and watched her knit.

"Grandma?" said Ivy.

"Yes, dear?"

"How come you forgave me so quickly?"

"Because *I've* been forgiven so many times," said Grandma.

Ivy rested her head on Grandma's shoulder. "I want to be a quick forgiver too," she said.

Grandma breathed a gentle sigh and said in a soft whisper,

"My, how Ivy has grown."

"Be gentle and ready to forgive;
never hold grudges.
Remember, the Lord forgave you."
Colossians 3:13

Can you remember?

What presents did Grandma give each child?

Which present broke another present?

How did Ivy show she was upset with Dustin?

How did Ivy feel in her heart before she forgave Dustin?

How did she feel inside after she forgave him?

What were Ivy and Dustin doing when she forgave him?

What do you think?

Why is it hard to forgive someone?

How does it hurt us when we don't forgive others?

How does it hurt other people?

What made it easier for Ivy to forgive her brother?

For what things have you been forgiven? Who forgave you?

Who needs your forgiveness?

A Word from the Author to Parents and Teachers

Years ago, our three-year-old son Nathan attempted a headstand as Jan and her teenage sister, Leslie, watched. Nathan had almost made it up when Leslie couldn't resist the urge to nudge him playfully. Over he went in a somersault.

Feeling a bit guilty, Aunt Leslie quickly apologized. Nathan said nothing.

"Would you like to tell Aunt Leslie that you forgive her?" Jan prodded.

Nathan stared blankly at his aunt.

"I really didn't mean for you to fall," Aunt Leslie tried to assure him. "It was an accident."

A cute smile crept across Nathan's face, and he wrapped his arms around her neck.

"I forgive you," he said with childlike innocence. "And when I knock you down, it will be an accident too, okay?"

We've all been knocked down plenty of times. Some offenses are completely accidental, others grossly thoughtless, and still others deliberate and malicious. To every known offense, we respond. One response option is to retaliate. Another common one is to withdraw, which often includes sulking and growing resentful. The noblest option—and usually the hardest—is to forgive.

In *Ivy's Icicle,* it is not my intent to analyze forgiveness. Quite honestly, I can't figure it out. Is it a feeling? a choice? Is it both, or perhaps even more? Is it only something *we* do, or is it something that must be done *in* us? Is it a step that leads to healing, or is it a sign that healing has taken place?

Simplistic formulas for forgiveness can trivialize pains that defy description. This story offers no formula, no explanation for forgiveness. Rather, I hope that *Ivy's Icicle* will simply foster it.

Like Ivy, I've found myself on both sides of offenses. Lots of offenses. Some have been purely accidental. Some were a result of horrendous inconsideration. Sadly, I admit that sometimes I have been deliberately mean. Yet, with each offense I experience a depth of forgiveness that leaves me speechless. It comes from the One of whom it is written, "O Lord, you are so good and kind, so ready to forgive, so full of mercy for all who ask your aid" (Psalm 86:5).

I've found that when I sincerely and sorrowfully admit my wrongs to Jesus Christ, He wipes that slate clean and gives me a fresh start with a renewed heart (1 John 1:9). Such mercy changes me. The recollection of the many times I've received His mercy melts my heart and enables me to forgive those who hurt me.

I pray that you will know the peace of living a forgiven and forgiving life.